To all who searched,
for your time and commitment,
humbly, thank you.

ISBN 978-1-71-439559-0
The Pug That Got Away
Copyright 2019 by Amy Soucie

All illustrations were created by @venail and consent has been given for commercial use.

Printed in Canada.

A haiku is a Japanese verse form most often composed, in English, of three unrhymed lines of five, seven, and five syllables. A haiku format was chosen to promote the creativity of the author and the imagination of the reader.

Round face, curly tail
Small, red fire hydrant tag
Otis is his name.

Cute, lovable pug
Mischievous and clever
Trouble follows him.

Wrinkly faced pug,
Needs extra eyes to watch him
Full of energy.

Caring for Otis
Packing his food, leash, and toys
Where is he going?

Leaving home today,
Vacation calls the family,
A kennel awaits.

Temporary home,
Bright lights, smooth floors, and loud noises
The door is closed and locked.

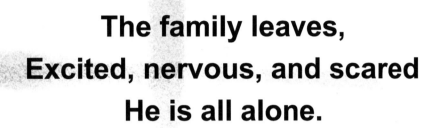

The family leaves,
Excited, nervous, and scared
He is all alone.

An honest mistake,
Unlocked door leads to escape,
Freedom awaits him.

Adventure begins,
Nothing looks familiar here,
Large, green soybean fields.

Old rusty silos,
Bridges, ditches, hot and dry
No water is near.

Construction and noise,
Dusty, gravel in his paws
Thirsty and tired.

How does he get home?
Running endlessly nowhere,
Afraid and alone.

Thirty volunteers
Chasing a pug in a field,
Running faster, but ...

Safety, warmth and food
Hiding spots abound everywhere,
Good thing he is small.

On the Greenway Trail,
Trees and leaves, shade from the sun
A quiet moment.

Bugs, birds and bunnies,
Exploring and learning fast
Raccoons, snakes and frogs.

A farm comes into view,
Off the beaten path - what now?
Light and love await.

His new friend, Lincoln,
Barking together at night,
He is not alone.

Getting tired now,
Where is his family?
Missing them and home.

Cat food and hot dogs,
Tricked him into a live trap
Dirty, wet and cold.

He wants to go home,
Thinking, when will he be found?
Sooner or later.

Humans approach me,
Spot my tiny red name tag
I'm finally found.

Mommy and Daddy,
Tears of joy, screaming, jumping
Car ride and cuddles.

Safe with my people,
Happiness and relief now
Off to the doctor's.

Eye drops and water,
Back at home with family
Worn out, sleepy, snuggling.

Nine lives like a cat
Lost but found, feeling better ...

A Happy Ending!

Otis Hamilton Soucie